Welcome to **ALADDIN QUIX!**

If you are looking for fast, fun-to-read stories with colorful characters, lots of kid-friendly humor, easy-to-follow action, entertaining story lines, and lively illustrations, then **ALADDIN QUIX** is for you!

But wait, there's more!

If you're also looking for stories with tables of contents; word lists; about-the-book questions; 64, 80, or 96 pages; short chapters; short paragraphs; and large fonts, then **ALADDIN QUIX** is *definitely* for you!

ALADDIN QUIX: The next step between ready to reads and longer, more challenging chapter books, for readers five to eight years old.

LOST AND FOUND

Read more ALADDIN QUIX books!

By Stephanie Calmenson

Our Principal Is a Frog!

Our Principal Is a Wolf!

Our Principal's in His Underwear!

Our Principal Breaks a Spell!

Our Principal's Wacky Wishes!

Our Principal Is a Spider!

Little Goddess Girls
By Joan Holub and Suzanne Williams

Book 1: *Athena & the Magic Land*

Book 2: *Persephone & the Giant Flowers*

Book 3: *Aphrodite & the Gold Apple*

Book 4: *Artemis & the Awesome Animals*

Mack Rhino, Private Eye

Book 1: *The Big Race Lace Case*

Book 2: *The Candy Caper Case*

Geeger the Robot

Book 1: *Geeger the Robot Goes to School*

GEEGER THE ROBOT

LOST AND FOUND

JARRETT LERNER

ILLUSTRATED BY

Serge
Seidlitz

ALADDIN QUIX

New York London Toronto Sydney New Delhi

ALADDIN QUIX

Simon & Schuster Children's Publishing Division

1230 Avenue of the Americas, New York, New York 10020

First Aladdin QUIX paperback edition January 2021

Text copyright © 2021 by Jarrett Lerner

Illustrations copyright © 2021 by Serge Seidlitz

Also available in an Aladdin QUIX hardcover edition.

All rights reserved, including the right of reproduction in whole or in part in any form.

ALADDIN and related logo are registered trademarks of Simon & Schuster, Inc.

For information about special discounts for bulk purchases, please contact Simon & Schuster Special Sales at 1-866-506-1949 or business@simonandschuster.com.

The Simon & Schuster Speakers Bureau can bring authors to your live event. For more information or to book an event contact the Simon & Schuster Speakers Bureau at 1-866-248-3049 or visit our website at www.simonspeakers.com.

Book designed by Karin Paprocki

The illustrations for this book were rendered digitally.

The text of this book was set in Archer Medium.

Manufactured in the United States of America 1120 OFF

2 4 6 8 10 9 7 5 3 1

Library of Congress Control Number 2020947426

ISBN 978-1-5344-5220-6 (hc)

ISBN 978-1-5344-5219-0 (pbk)

ISBN 978-1-5344-5221-3 (eBook)

For Greg and Jim,

friends as good as any

Cast of Characters

Geeger: a very hungry robot

DIGEST-O-TRON 5000: a machine that turns the food Geeger eats into electricity

Fudge the Hamster: Ms. Bork's class pet

Ms. Bork: Geeger's teacher

Tillie: a student at Geeger's school, and Geeger's first new friend

Arjun, Olivia, Mac, Sidney, Suzie, Gabe, Roxy, Raul: other kids in Geeger's class

Contents

Meet Geeger

Geeger is a robot. A very, very hungry robot.

Geeger was **constructed** in a laboratory by a team of scientists. Then he was sent to a town called Amblerville. There, Geeger eats all the food that the rest of the townspeople don't want.

Rotten eggs, moldy bread, mushy fruit—you name it!

Geeger has a brain, just like you. The only difference is that Geeger's brain is made up of wires. Your brain, meanwhile, is made up of . . . well, gooey brain stuff.

Most of the time, Geeger's brain tells him to do just one thing: **EAT! EAT! EAT! EAT! EAT!**

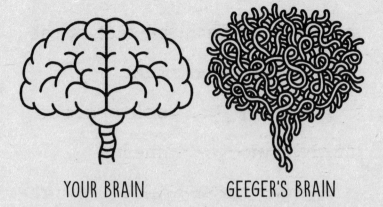

YOUR BRAIN   GEEGER'S BRAIN

At the end of every day, Geeger plugs himself into his **DIGEST-O-TRON 5000**. The machine sucks up all the food that Geeger has eaten and turns it into electricity. The electricity then helps power the town!

Now and again, Geeger gets

confused and eats things he's not supposed to.

Like forks.

And batteries.

And toaster ovens.

When Geeger does that, the DIGEST-O-TRON lets him know. The machine's lights flash. Its sirens scream. **WEE-oOoOo! WEE-oOoOo! WEE-oOoOo!**

Not too long ago, Geeger started something very new. He enrolled in school!

Geeger has now been going to Amblerville Elementary School for two whole weeks. That's not very long—but Geeger has already learned **LOTS**.

For instance:

Geeger has learned that Amblerville is a town on the planet Earth, and that Earth spins in circles around the sun.

He's also learned that the sun and Earth are part of a **galaxy**, and that *that* galaxy is called the Milky Way—but *not* because there's any actual *milk* in it.

One other thing that Geeger has learned:

It's not just kids and teachers (and one robot!) who spend their days at Amblerville Elementary School. There are *animals*, too!

Like **Fudge the Hamster, Ms. Bork**'s class pet.

Geeger is a **BIG** fan of Fudge. The hamster is cute. And fuzzy. And cuddly. And sometimes,

he climbs up Geeger's arm and
onto the top of the robot's head.
There, the little guy runs laps

around Geeger's light bulb. The hamster's tiny, fast-moving feet always make Geeger's wires tingle with delight.

Also, Fudge has *great* taste in food. His favorite thing to eat is old, brown, mushy bananas. And Geeger loves old, brown, mushy bananas too!

Something else that Geeger has learned is that being a student requires **LOTS** and **LOTS** (and ***LOTS!***) of energy. Which means it's more important than ever that Geeger starts his day off right with a good breakfast.

And so Geeger screws a brand-new light bulb into the top of his head and makes his way to the kitchen.

2

Breakfast Time

Geeger goes bonkers as soon as he enters the kitchen. He sees all the buckets and barrels and cartons and containers of spoiled and rotten and stale and **expired** food gathered there.

EAT! EAT! EAT! EAT! HURRY UP AND EAT!

his brain tells him.

So Geeger eats!

First he has:

> three boxes of crackers (stale)
> six avocados (rotten)
> and
> two and a half pounds of sliced Swiss
> cheese (moldy)

"**ECK-*sep*-TION-AL**," Geeger says, slinging the last slice of cheese into his stomach. That's

Robot for **"exceptional,"** which means: *yum!*

But Geeger is still hungry.

So he eats a little more:

15 pancakes (slightly moldy)

nine apples (soft and mealy)

and

11 eggs (rotten and STINKY)

"ECK-*squiz***-IT,"** Geeger says, cracking the last of the nasty

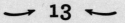

eggs and dumping it into his guts. That's Robot for **"exquisite,"** which means: *super yummy!*

But Geeger is *still* hungry. So he eats **A LOT** more:

four grapefruits (moldy)

one bag of spinach (wilted)

two zucchinis (slimy)

one can of kidney beans (expired)

three cans of cannellini beans (VERY expired)

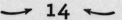

one TV remote control

(missing several buttons)

seven peanut butter granola bars (stale)

two boxes of cereal (staler than stale)

and

one pack of rice cakes (pretty much the

stalest thing in the whole wide world)

"**ECK**-*stror*-**DIN**-**AIR**-*eee*,"
Geeger says. That's Robot for
"**extraordinary**," which means:
holy cow, was that yummy!

Geeger slams the door to his stomach shut and is just about to **declare** breakfast a success and get ready to go to school.

But then a strange feeling comes over him.

It's a feeling he's been experiencing more and more lately, ever since he started going to Amblerville Elementary School.

It's a feeling that he might have accidentally just done something wrong....

Geeger looks around the kitchen.

But nothing appears out of place.

"HMMMMM...," Geeger says. Which is just Robot for: *hmmmm.*

All of a sudden, the light bulb on top of Geeger's head blinks brightly.

Geeger has an idea.

Opening the door to his stomach, Geeger peers inside. And past the pancakes, over the avocados, and across from the cannellini beans, he sees it—a TV remote, missing several buttons and now splattered with rotten egg and cracker crumbs.

If Geeger could blush, he would be blushing right now.

He's just glad he's not at school, where Ms. Bork and all his classmates could see that he ate something he shouldn't have—*again*.

Geeger sets the TV remote on

the counter. Then he tells himself that he shouldn't be too upset. After all, he realized that he'd eaten something he shouldn't have just a couple minutes after he did it. It could've been worse.

It could've been **WAY** worse....

Not wanting to think these thoughts any longer, Geeger grabs his backpack and heads for the door.

3

One Whole Week

As soon as Geeger steps out his front door, he hears some-one shout, **"GEEGER! Over here!"**

Geeger looks up and sees **Tillie**. She's waiting for him right there on the sidewalk, just like she has every day since Geeger's first day of school.

Tillie smiles, and the light bulb atop Geeger's head twinkles and shines.

"*Goood* **MOR-NING, TILL-***eee*," Geeger says. He joins her on the sidewalk, and together they make their way toward Amblerville Elementary School.

"It *is* a good morning," Tillie says. She grins up at Geeger.

"And do you know why?"

Geeger looks around. The sun is shining. There are a few big, white, fluffy clouds in the sky.

The trees are bending in a gentle breeze, and Geeger has his best

friend in the whole entire Milky Way by his side. Geeger can think of several reasons why it is a very good morning.

But before Geeger can share any of these reasons with Tillie, she throws her arms up into the air and declares:

"It's been ONE WHOLE WEEK since you ate something you shouldn't have! *That's* why it's such a good morning. You should be so proud of yourself, Geeger. *I'm* **so proud of you!**"

The light bulb atop Geeger's head—which has been shining all this time—suddenly goes dark.

Geeger can't help but think about the TV remote that he accidentally shoved into his stomach earlier this morning.

"Geeger," Tillie says. "Is something wrong?"

Geeger gives his head a shake, hoping to knock his unhappy thoughts out of it. Then he turns his attention to something very, very happy.

"*Loook* **AT THIS**," he tells Tillie, shifting his backpack so that he can reach into it. And out from the biggest pocket he pulls . . .

. . . a pair of old, brown, mushy
bananas!

Tillie's face lights up.

"Are those for Fudge?!" she asks.

Geeger nods.

"He's going to LOVE them!" Tillie says.

"I *hooope* **SO**," says Geeger.

"I *know* so," says Tillie.

Geeger drops the bananas back into his backpack, feeling a bit better about the day ahead of him.

A Pair of Bananas

Ms. Bork's classroom is already crowded by the time Geeger and Tillie get there.

Together, the friends head for their cubbies to put away their backpacks. But before he tucks *his* backpack away, Geeger removes one of the two old, brown, mushy bananas that he brought to school.

Geeger hides the banana behind his back, then starts toward the back of the room, to where Fudge the Hamster lives.

On his way, Geeger high-fives **Arjun** and waves to **Olivia**.

He fist-bumps **Mac** and smiles at **Sidney**.

He says **"HIII"** to **Suzie** and greets **Gabe**.

He low-fives **Roxy** and nods to **Raul**.

And then, at last, Geeger arrives. He steps right up to the big glass case with the brightly colored, hamster-size tunnels **jutting** out of it.

Fudge **scurries** over to the front of his case the second he spots Geeger. He rises up onto his back legs and says,

SQUEEEEEAK! SQUEAK!

SQUEAK-SQUEAK! SQUEEEAK!

Geeger grins at the hamster. He keeps his hand holding the old, mushy, brown banana behind his back, but reaches his other hand down into the case.

Fudge climbs aboard and quickly scurries up Geeger's arm and onto his shoulder. There, the hamster rises onto his hind legs and *leaps*, landing on the side of Geeger's head and clinging to it with his itsy-bitsy claws.

A beat later, Fudge is up on top of Geeger's head, running laps around the robot's light bulb. The **sensation** makes Geeger's wires tingle. The big battery in his chest gets warm. He feels happy and calm.

Finally, the hamster climbs back down and into his cage.

At which point Geeger tells Fudge, **"CHECK THIS *ouuut.*"**

Geeger pulls the old, mushy, brown banana out from behind his back.

Fudge sees the piece of overripe fruit and starts zipping around in circles.

He's moving so fast, his paws kick up the wood shavings that his case is filled with.

Geeger giggles, then unpeels the banana and breaks it in two. There's now a hamster-size piece for Fudge and a robot-size piece for Geeger.

Reaching back into the case, Geeger picks up Fudge. He holds on to the hamster while the fuzzy little guy nibbles away at the fruit.

And even though he just ate a gigantic breakfast, Geeger can't help but get hungry at the sight of the piece of banana resting in his other hand. Before he even realizes what he's doing, he tosses the thing down his throat.

"**ECK**-*sell*—" Geeger starts to say. But he doesn't get the word out before Ms. Bork calls, "Okay, class! **Time to start our day!**"

Geeger knows what that means. Two seconds later, he's sitting in his seat. He has his notebook out on his desk and a pencil in his hand. He's ready to start the day!

Ms. Bork sees, and gives Geeger a smile.

"Today," she tells the class, "we'll continue learning about the weather. Can anyone—"

"EEEEK!"

Everyone spins around to look at Suzie. She was the one who shrieked.

"Suzie?" says Ms. Bork. "What's wrong?"

"Look!" she says, pointing at the hamster case. **"Fudge is missing!"**

5

Chaos in the Classroom

There's **chaos** in Ms. Bork's class.

Everyone is up out of their seats and hurrying over to get a look at Fudge's case.

"Where is he?!" cries Arjun.

"What do we do?!" shouts Raul.

Tillie reaches into the case and sifts through the wood shavings.

Roxy and Sidney search all the tunnels.

Geeger stands apart from the others, feeling scared and sad and confused.

"What if he gets lost and we don't ever find him?" asks Suzie.

"What if he gets into

the basement and has to battle the **mutant** rats who live down there?!" asks Gabe.

"Class!" calls Ms. Bork. "Quiet down, please."

It takes a moment, but then everyone is silent.

Ms. Bork takes a deep breath.

"First of all," she says, "there are no mutant rats in the basement. And we *will* find Fudge. We just need to be **logical** about it. He was in his case when I got to school this morning. That was only twenty minutes ago. Did anyone see him after that?"

"I checked to make sure he had water," Olivia says.

"I gave him a quick chin scratch," says Mac.

Geeger knows he should tell Ms. Bork that he visited with Fudge right before class started. But he can't move. He can't speak. He is frozen with worry and fear.

Suzie clears her throat.

"Yes, Suzie?" says Ms. Bork. "Do you have something to share?"

"I . . . ," Suzie begins. "I saw Geeger feeding Fudge an old banana. It was just a minute ago."

Every pair of eyes in the classroom turns toward Geeger.

"Geeger," Ms. Bork says. "Is there anything you want to tell us?"

"**WELL . . . ,**" Geeger says. "**I—I WAS** *feee*-**DING FUDGE A BA-NA-***naaa*. **AND THEN I GOT HUN-***greee*. **SO I HAD SOME**

BA-NA-*naaa*. AND I MUST HAVE LOST TRACK *of* TIME. CLASS *beee*-GAN. AND I . . . I DO *nooot* RE-MEM-BER. THE NEXT THING I *knooow*, I WAS AT *myyy* DESK."

The rest of the kids look around at one another.

Then Gabe says, "Geeger . . . you didn't *eat* Fudge, did you?"

Before Geeger can react, Tillie nudges him aside and leaps in front of him.

"Geeger would **NEVER** do

that!" she shouts at Gabe. "Geeger loves Fudge more than any of us do! More than all of us COMBINED!"

"Class, enough!" cries Ms. Bork. "Standing around pointing fingers is *not* going to help us find Fudge. If he was here just a minute ago, he can't have gotten far. Quickly, now—everyone, look around for him."

Geeger still feels frozen.

But Tillie takes hold of his arm and pulls him along.

6

Geeger Gets an Idea

The class fans out across the room, pairs of kids **staking** out different areas to search. Tillie yanks Geeger away from all the others.

"I can't believe they think

you'd ever *eat* Fudge," she hisses.

Geeger doesn't answer.

Instead he taps a finger against the door to his stomach.

"**MAY-***beee* . . . ," he says. "**MAY-***beee*, **JUST IN CASE**, *weee* **SHOULD CHECK**?"

Suddenly, Tillie seems more upset with Geeger than she does with the other kids.

"Absolutely *not*, Geeger," she says. "There's no need. You did NOT eat Fudge. You probably just forgot to put him back in his case."

Tillie looks up at Geeger like she's waiting for him to agree with her.

So Geeger says, **"PROB-UB-** *leee . . ."* Even though he doesn't totally believe it.

Tillie turns to face the rest of the room.

"Okay," she says. "Let's be logical about this, like Ms. Bork said. You look high, Geeger, and I'll look low."

Tillie drops to her knees and begins crawling around on the carpet.

She peers into the gap between the bottom of the bookshelf and the floor. She checks behind the bins where Ms. Bork keeps all her art supplies.

She looks under every:

- backpack
- notebook
- lunch bag
- sweatshirt.

Geeger watches her, feeling more scared and sad and confused by the second.

"How's it going up there, Geeger?" Tillie calls to him.

"Ummmmm . . . ," Geeger says. Then he hurries up and gets searching.

He **examines** each and every bookshelf, and even slides out some of the books to make sure Fudge didn't somehow get behind them.

He inspects:
- the scissors bin
- the glue stick bin
- the construction paper bin
- the crayon bin
- the marker bin
- the googly-eye-and-glitter bin.

He **scans** all the desks nearby,

lifting up notebooks and binders and pencil holders and papers in case Fudge decided to squeeze himself under there.

But the hamster isn't in any of those places.

And none of the other kids are having any better luck.

"He's not in the coat closet!" calls Arjun.

"Or in the floor mat cabinet!" Sidney adds.

"I found that eraser I lost last week!" says Gabe. "But not Fudge . . ."

One by one, all the kids turn to look at Geeger.

Geeger knows what they're thinking, because *he's* thinking the same thing. The kids have searched just about every place in the classroom that a missing hamster could be—*except* for Geeger's stomach!

"Geeger . . . ," Ms. Bork says.

Geeger looks down at the door to his stomach.

But before he can open it, Tillie climbs to her feet and comes to his side.

"Geeger loves Fudge," she tells the class. "He would never do a thing to hurt him. The fact that he brought Fudge those two old, mushy, brown bananas this morning proves that. He *saved* them for Fudge, because he—"

BZZZZZT!

The light bulb atop Geeger's head **illuminates**. It's glowing as brightly as it ever has before. Geeger has got an IDEA!

Noticing the glow over his head, Tillie says, "What is it, Geeger?! What is it?!"

"I BROUGHT *twooo* BAN-AN-*aaas* THIS MOR-*niiing*," he says. "BUT I ON-*leee* GAVE FUDGE ONE."

Tillie grins, then aims her eyes over toward Geeger's backpack, tucked in his cubby on the other side of the room.

7

Squeeeeeak

Geeger leads the way across the room and over to his backpack. Tillie is right on his heels. Just a moment after they arrive at Geeger's cubby, the rest of the class is there too, with Ms. Bork at the front of the group. They gather around to get a look at Geeger and Tillie.

"What's going on?" asks Raul.

"Why did we just run over here?" wonders Roxy.

"I think I lost my eraser again," says Gabe.

Then Tillie says, "*Shhh!* Listen!"

Everyone quiets down, and the sound they hear is unmistakable.

"**SQUEEEEEAK!**

SQUEAK-SQUEAK-SQUEAK SQUEAK SQUEAK-SQUEAK SQUEEEEEEEAK!"

Slowly, carefully, Geeger pulls his backpack out from his cubby. And slowly, carefully, Tillie reaches a hand into the backpack's biggest pocket.

Then she giggles.

"That tickles, Fudge!" she cries.

She pulls her hand out of the backpack, and there, sitting in her palm, is Fudge, bits of old, mushy, brown banana caught in his thin little whiskers.

Ms. Bork breathes a sigh of relief. Then she takes Fudge from Tillie and carries him to his case.

Turning back to Geeger, she says, "I'm sorry, Geeger. For a moment there, I doubted you. I was worried about Fudge, and **anxious** to find him. And so I thought you might've done something that, when I'm thinking clearly, I know you'd never do. I shouldn't have done that. I know you better by now."

"Yeah," says Suzie. "I'm sorry too, Geeger."

"So am I," says Gabe.

Before anyone else can apologize, Geeger says, **"IT'S OH**-*kaaay.* **I DOUBT-ED MY-SELF** *tooo.*"

Tillie puffs out her chest and jabs a finger at herself.

"*I* didn't," she says. "And *that's* why it's a good thing you've got me around."

Across the room, Fudge rises up onto his back legs and says, "*SQUEAK SQUEAK SQUEAK SQUEEEEEEEEEEEEEEEAK!*"

8

Lost and Found

Ms. Bork decides that the class's lesson on weather can wait a little bit. She declares the next ten minutes Fudge Time!

Sidney and Suzie shove aside all the desks.

Roxy and Raul grab the floor mats from the cabinet, and then Arjun, Olivia, and Mac help them place the mats in a big circle in the center of the room.

Ms. Bork helps Gabe look for the eraser that he lost, then found, then lost again.

And Geeger and Tillie are in charge of getting Fudge.

Carefully, Tillie lifts the hamster out of his case. Meanwhile, Geeger reaches high onto the shelf above and grabs some of Fudge's favorite toys.

Once everyone is on their mats, Ms. Bork gives Tillie a thumbs-up.

Tillie lowers her hands toward the floor, and Fudge leaps off her fingertips and instantly begins zipping about.

He:

• zigzags

• darts in circles

• climbs over legs and feet and into laps

• even, at one point, **ventures** all the way up on top of Ms. Bork's head!

It's a very exciting ten minutes.

And the whole rest of the day is pretty exciting too.

Just like every day, Geeger learns **LOTS**.

For instance, did you know that clouds are made up of *trillions* of little drops of water, or that some clouds can weigh more than *one million pounds*?

Geeger learns tons of other interesting things about clouds and storms and the climate. But as he's walking home from school with Tillie, Geeger decides that the coolest thing he learned all day was about her, Tillie, his best friend.

He learned that she believes in him just as much as he believes in himself—and sometimes, even more! And when you're lucky enough to have a friend like that, it makes every day a little bit brighter.

Word List

anxious (ANK•shuss): Very worried or nervous

chaos (KAY•oss): Extreme craziness and confusion

constructed (con•STRUCK•ted): Built, made, or put together

declare (dee•CLAYR): To say something strongly

examines (ehk•ZAM•ins): Looks at very, very closely

exceptional (ehk•SEP•shun•ull): Very good

exquisite (eck•SQUIZ•it): Very, very good

expired (eck•SPY•erd): No longer fresh or good for eating

extraordinary (eck•STRAWR•din•air•ee): Very, very, *very* good

galaxy (GAL•eck•see): Any of the large groups of stars and other matter found throughout the universe

grateful (GRAYT•full): Happy and thankful for something or someone

illuminates (ih•LOOM•ihn•ates): Lights up

jutting (JUT•ing): Poking out at an angle

logical (LAH•jih•kull): Clear; makes sense

mutant (MYOO•tint): A plant or animal that is much different from the usual way of being

scans (SKANZ): Looks over or reads quickly

scurries (SKUR•eez): Hurries or moves quickly

sensation (sen•SAY•shun): A feeling your body experiences with its senses

staking out (STAY•king OWT): Claiming as one's own

ventures (VEN•churs): Goes somewhere difficult

Questions

1. Geeger is excited about all he's learned at school. What's one of the coolest things that *you've* learned at school?

2. What does Geeger put in his backpack to bring to school for Fudge?

3. Ms. Bork tells her students that they should be *logical* in their search for Fudge. What does she mean by that?

4. There are times when Tillie believes in Geeger even more than he believes in himself. Do you have someone who believes in you? Does having them believe in you help you believe in yourself?

5. There are several kids in Geeger's class. List as many of their names as you can.

6. At the end of the story, Geeger feels very **grateful** to have a friend as good as Tillie. Who or what are *you* grateful for?

From the authors of the bestselling *Goddess Girls* books
comes a new series of magical adventures with

Little GODDESS Girls!

**Athena &
the Magic Land**

**Persephone &
the Giant Flowers**

**Aphrodite &
the Gold Apple**

**Artemis &
the Awesome Animals**

EBOOK EDITIONS ALSO AVAILABLE

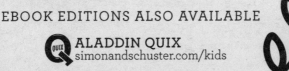

ALADDIN QUIX
simonandschuster.com/kids

Join the kids of PS 88 and

Principal Bundy

in their *wacky* and *silly* stories!